REICH   Illustrations by **RAÚL COLÓN**

PASS THE BABY

NEAL PORTER BOOKS
HOLIDAY HOUSE / NEW YORK

The author would like to thank the Bank Street Writers Lab.

Neal Porter Books

Text copyright © 2023 by Susanna Reich
Illustrations copyright © 2023 by Raúl Colón
All Rights Reserved
HOLIDAY HOUSE is registered in the U.S. Patent and Trademark Office.
Printed and bound in June 2023 at RR Donnelley, Dongguan, China.
The artwork for this book was created on Fabriano paper with watercolors, Prismacolor pencils, and lithographic crayons.
Book design by Jennifer Browne
www.holidayhouse.com
First Edition
1 3 5 7 9 10 8 6 4 2

Library of Congress Cataloging-in-Publication Data

Names: Reich, Susanna, author. | Colón, Raúl, illustrator.
Title: Pass the baby / by Susanna Reich ; illustrated by Raúl Colón.
Description: First edition. | New York : Holiday House, [2023] | "A Neal
Porter book." | Audience: Ages 4 to 8. | Audience: Grades K–1. |
Summary: "A delightful meal with a big extended family becomes a
free-for-all when one particularly excitable baby joins the fun"—
Provided by publisher.
Identifiers: LCCN 2022038049 | ISBN 9780823450855 (hardcover)
Subjects: CYAC: Stories in rhyme. | Family life—Fiction. | Racially mixed
families—Fiction. | LCGFT: Stories in rhyme. | Picture books.
Classification: LCC PZ8.3.R2654 Pas 2023 | DDC [E]—dc23
LC record available at https://lccn.loc.gov/2022038049

ISBN: 978-0-8234-5085-5 (hardcover)

To Livia, Frida, and Karen, with love —S.R.

For sweet baby Camden, who's had his share of being passed around —R.C.

Family dinner, set the table,
forks and spoons and napkins too.
Knives and plates and water glasses,
flowers, candles, bright and new.
Wait a minute, where's the baby?
Someone's playing peekaboo!

Fill the glasses, lots of ice,
fold the napkins nice and neat.
Call the guests to gather round,
grab a chair and take a seat.
Baby's fussing, must be hungry.
Hurry up, it's time to eat!

Baby, baby, pass the baby!

Baby wants a little bite.
Pass the baby round the table,
filled with faces shining bright.

Grandma sets out special dishes: pickles, olives, black-eyed peas.

Papi's making guacamole,   Mommy's busy grating cheese.

Baby wants a little laptime.
Hold her tight but do not squeeze.

Sister pours the lemonade,

Tía lights the candlesticks,

Grandpa takes a giant helping,

Grandma shares her latest pix.

Baby, baby, so excited.
Watch out for her little kicks!

Sister drips a saucy trickle,
Tío likes the guacamole,
Papi needs an enchilada,
Doggie steals a ravioli.
Baby's playing with a meatball.
It's a game of roly-poly.

Baby, baby, pass the baby!

Baby wants a little bite.
Pass the baby round the table,
filled with faces shining bright.

Everyplace that baby sits,
Doggie follows underneath,
lapping up the little morsels,
chewing, chewing with his teeth.
Papi thinks that Doggie's helpful,
Mommy says he's just a thief.

Baby takes some mashed banana,
flings it at the kitchen door,
bangs her spoon upon the table,
dribbles juice upon the floor.
Dripping, dropping, there's no stopping.
Give the baby more,

more,

MORE!

Mommy slices cherry cheesecake,
Grandma cuts the peanut pie,
Tío scoops vanilla ice cream,
Doggie's eating on the sly.
Baby's piling cake and cookies,
very, very, VERY high.

Doggie finds the crusty crumbs,
licks them up with great success.
Baby spills a cup of coffee,
right on Grandma's fancy dress.
Everybody grab a napkin.
Baby's made a great big mess!

Baby, baby, pass the baby!

Baby wants a little bite.
Pass the baby round the table,
'til it's time to say good night.

Papi picks up plates and platters,
Mommy says it's time for bed,
Sister wails for cozy nightgown,
Doggie nibbles gingerbread.
Baby dumps the sugar bowl,
upside down on dolly's head.

All the guests are so exhausted.
Soon they'll have to say goodbye.
Eyes are closing, Grandma's dozing,
stars are twinkling in the sky.
Doggie naps beneath the table.
Baby plays with Grandpa's tie.

Baby, baby, pass the baby!

Oops—the grown-ups are asleep.
Snoozing, snoring, they're so boring,
everyone is counting sheep. . . .

All the guests are so exhausted.
Soon they'll have to say goodbye.
Eyes are closing, Grandma's dozing,
stars are twinkling in the sky.
Doggie naps beneath the table.
Baby plays with Grandpa's tie.

Baby, baby, pass the baby!

Oops—the grown-ups are asleep.
Snoozing, snoring, they're so boring,
everyone is counting sheep. . . .

But you and baby keep on playing.
Shhh, you mustn't make a peep!